I Spy

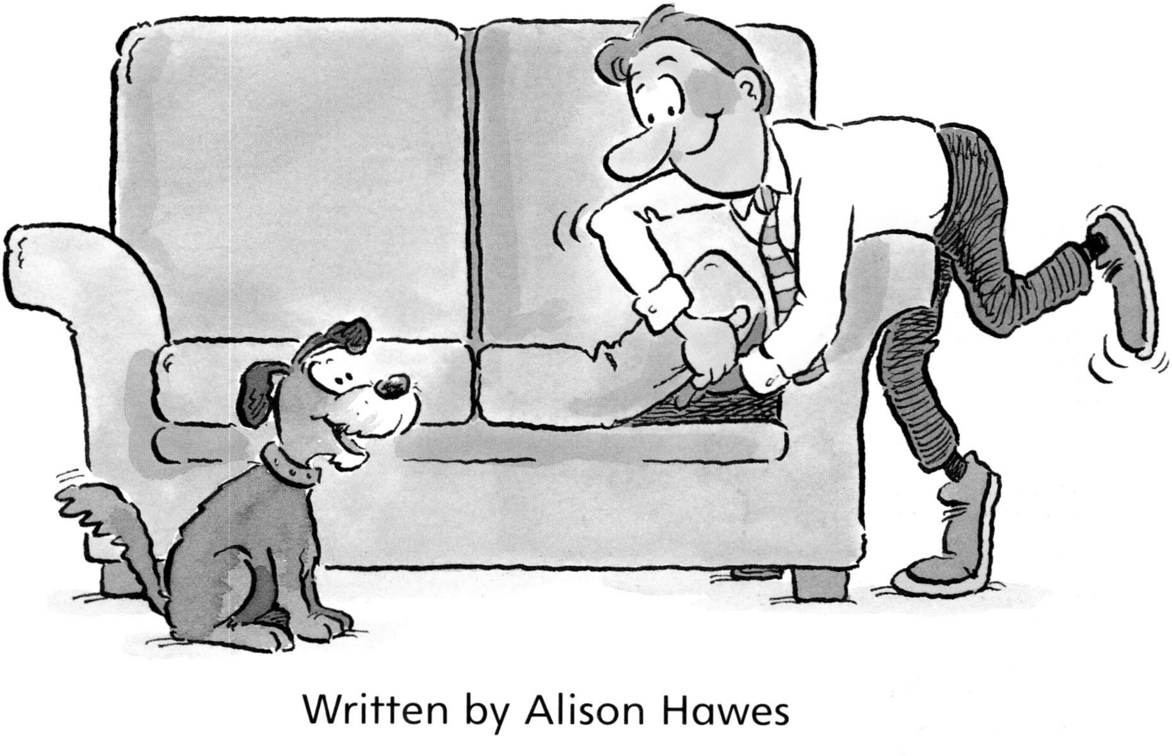

Written by Alison Hawes

Illustrated by Andy Hammond

I spy my lost car.

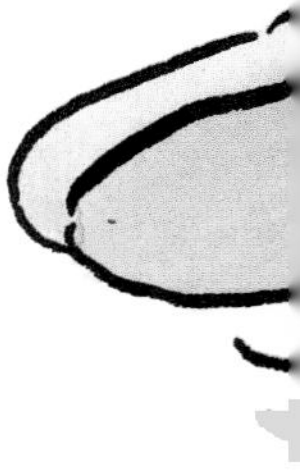

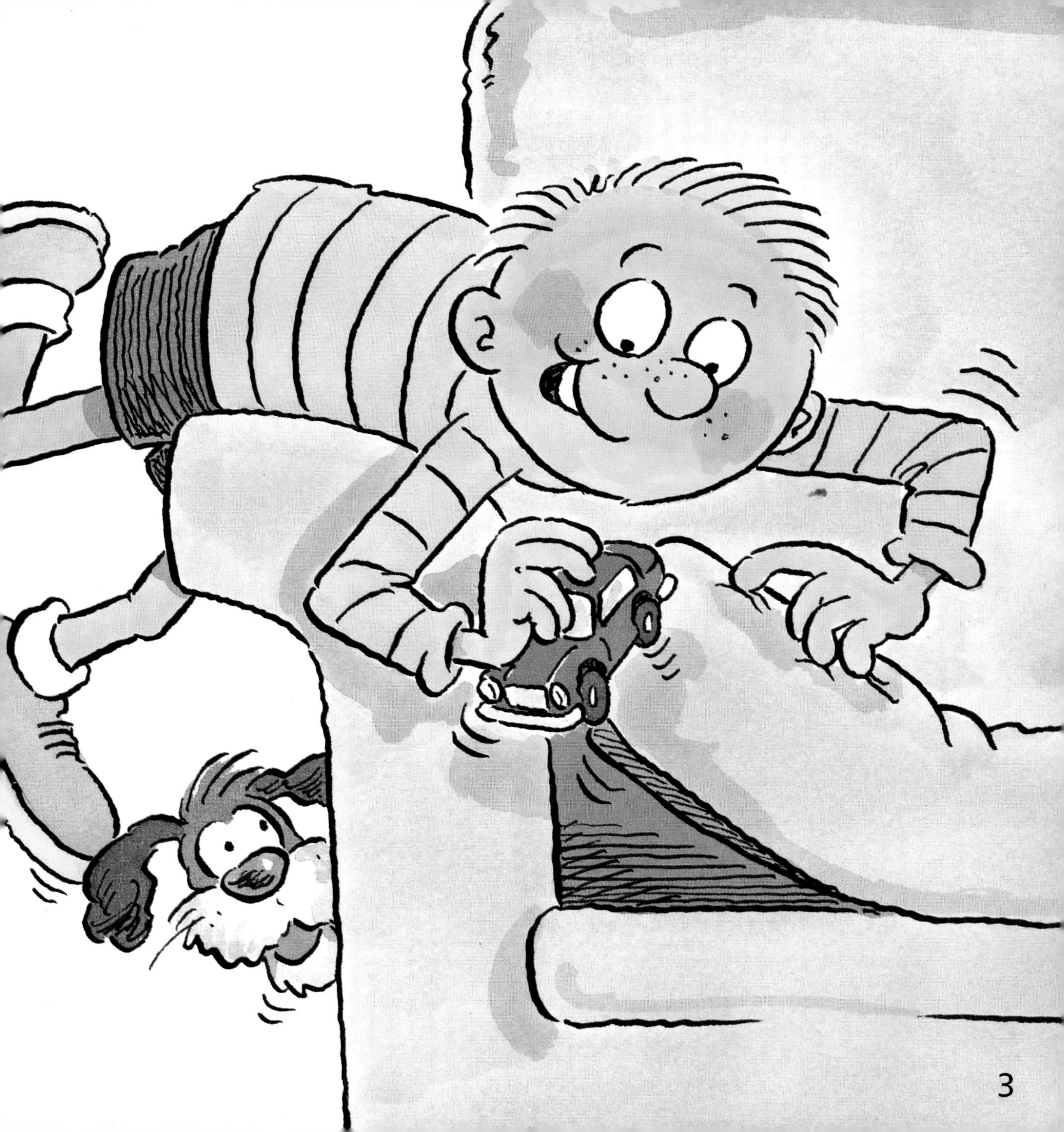

I spy my lost spoon.

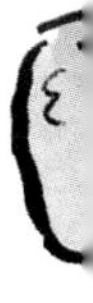

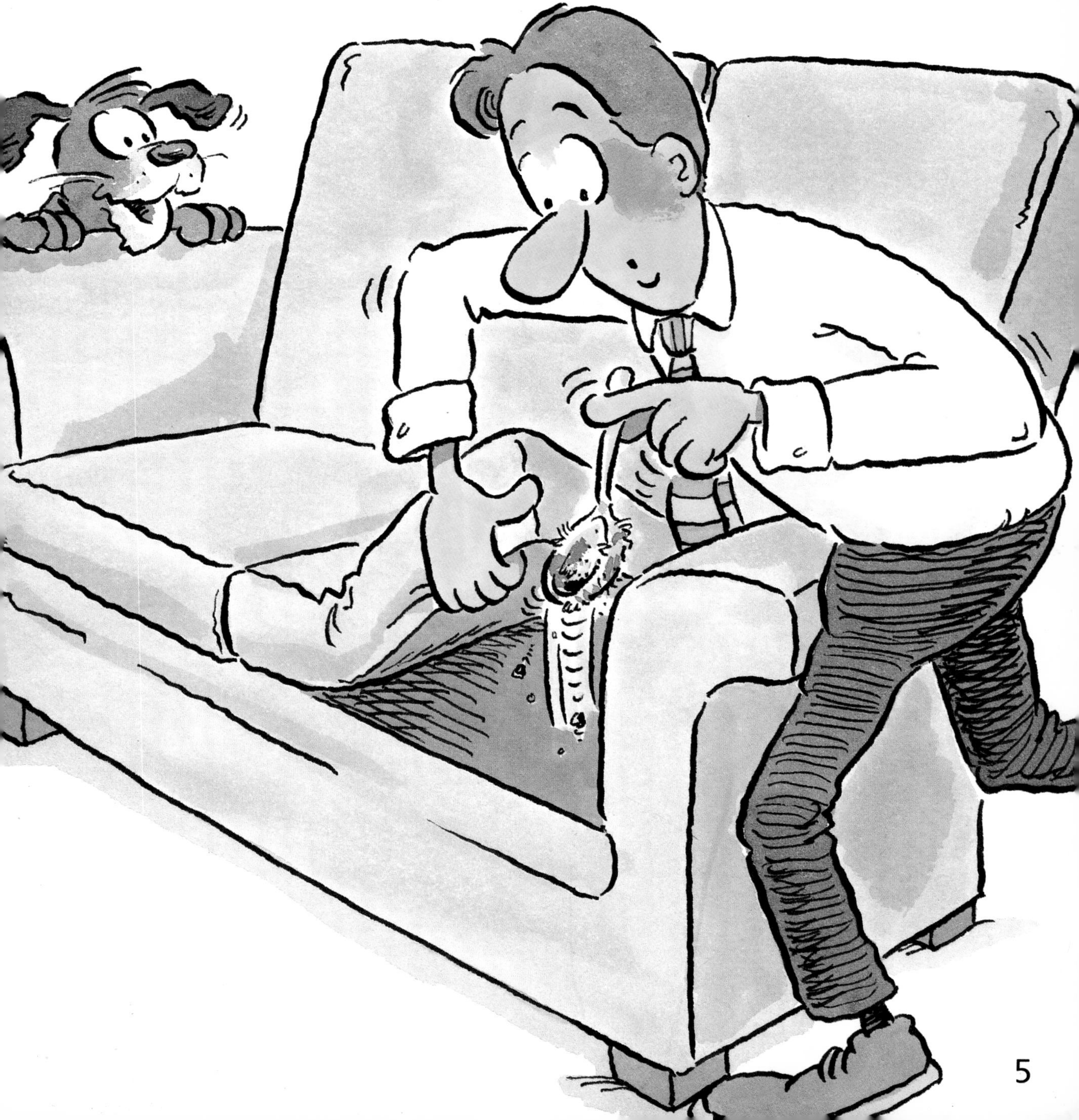

I spy my lost candy.

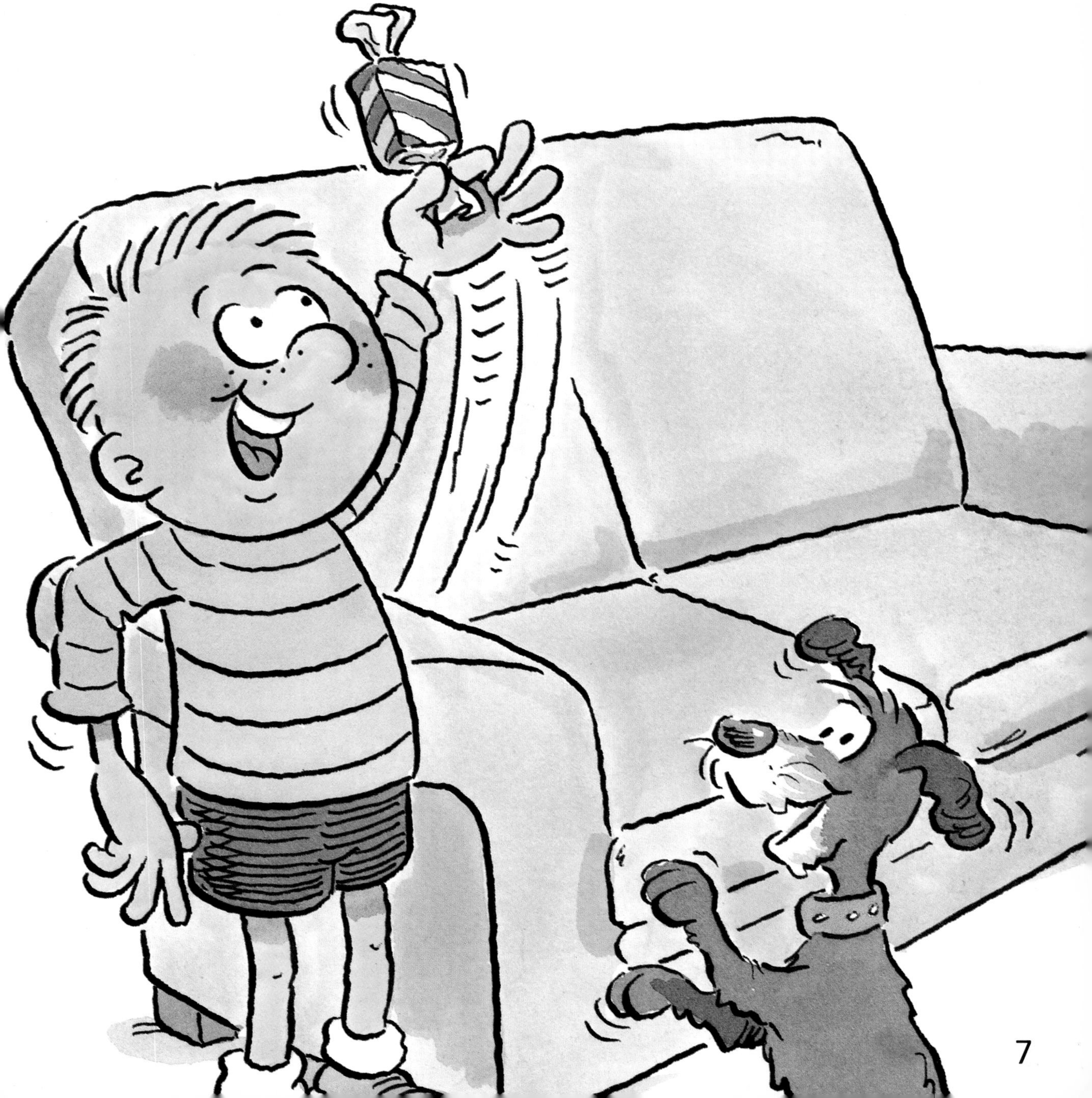

I spy my lost sock.

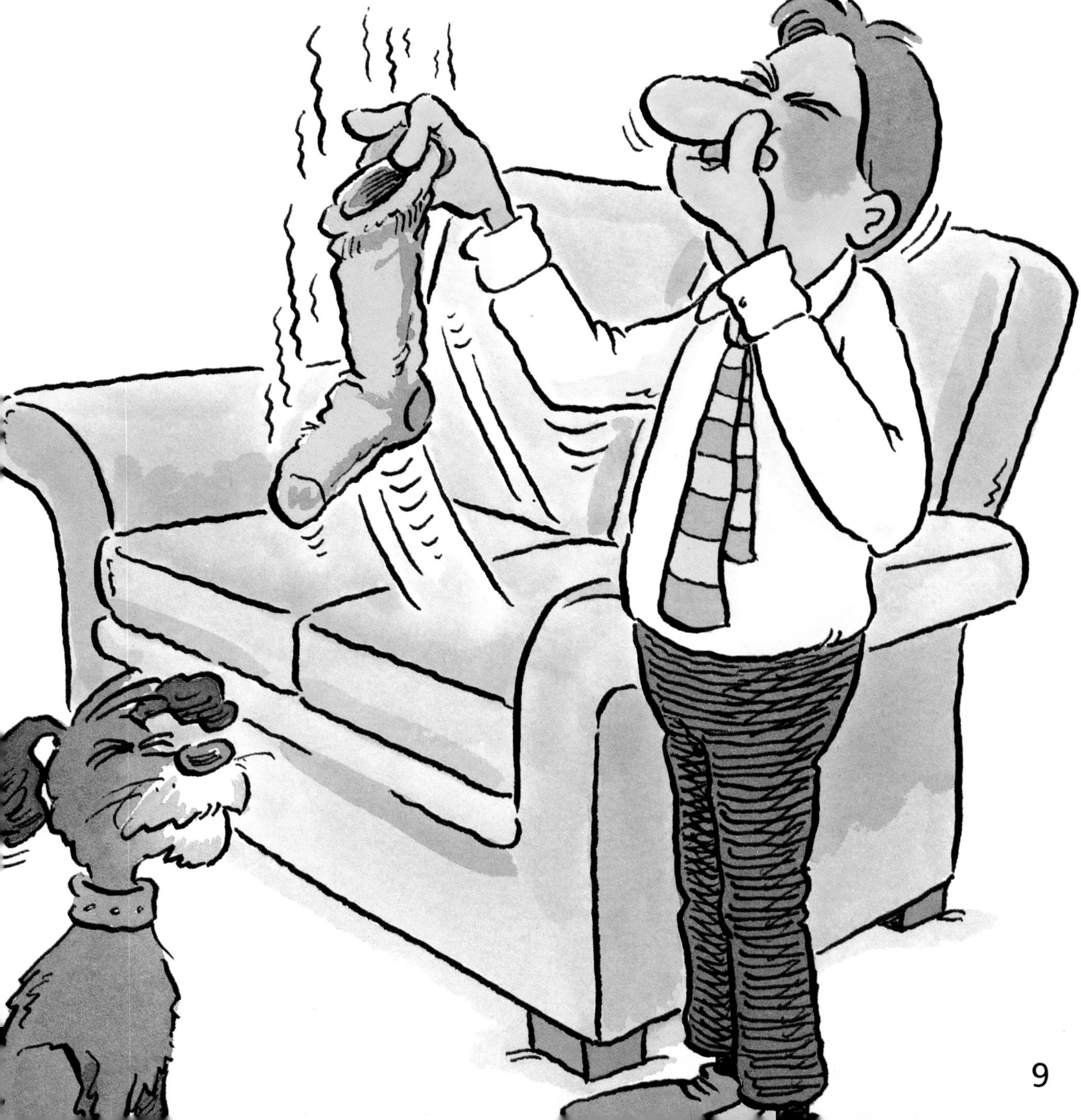

I spy my lost dime.

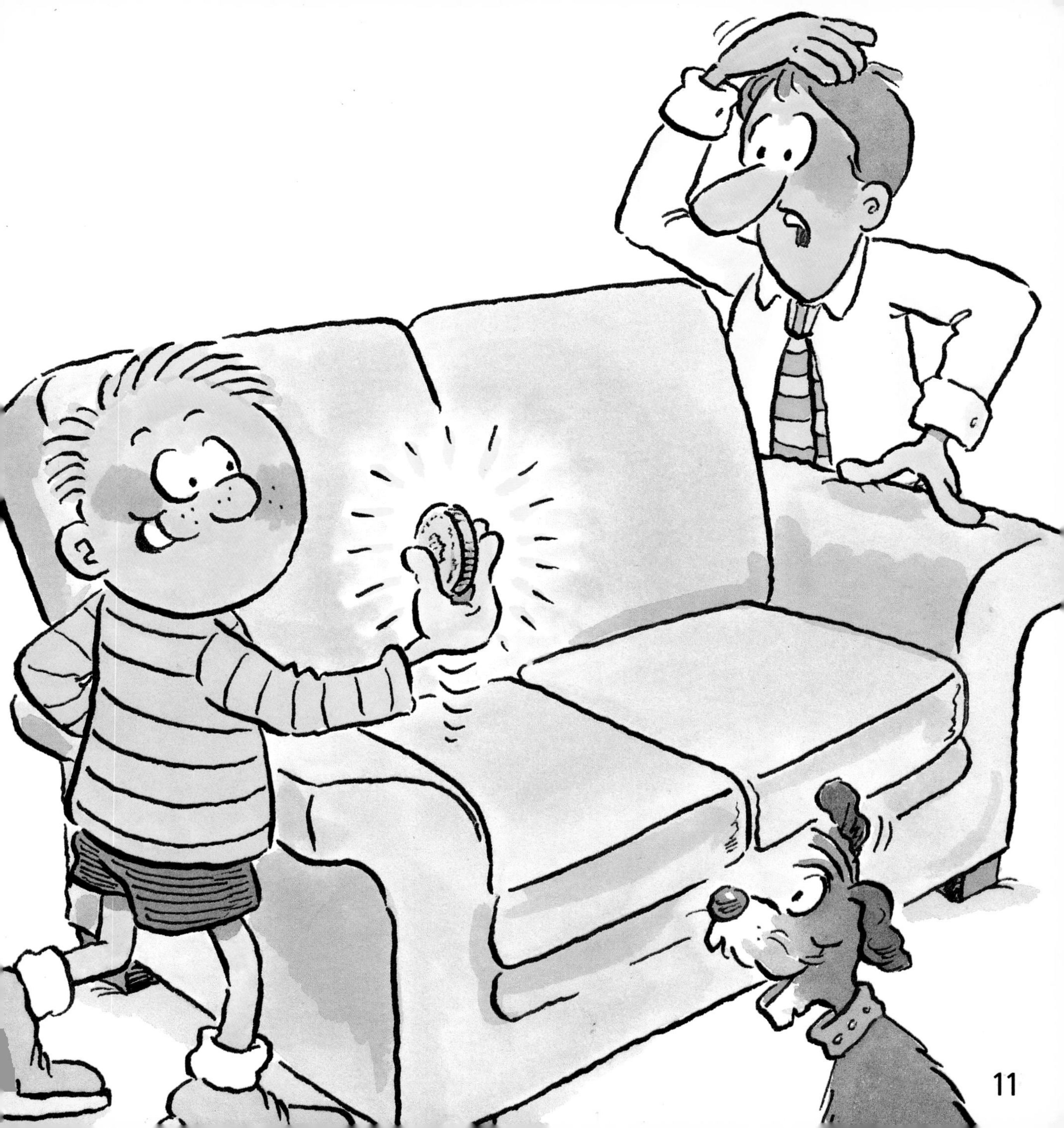

I spy my lost sandwich.

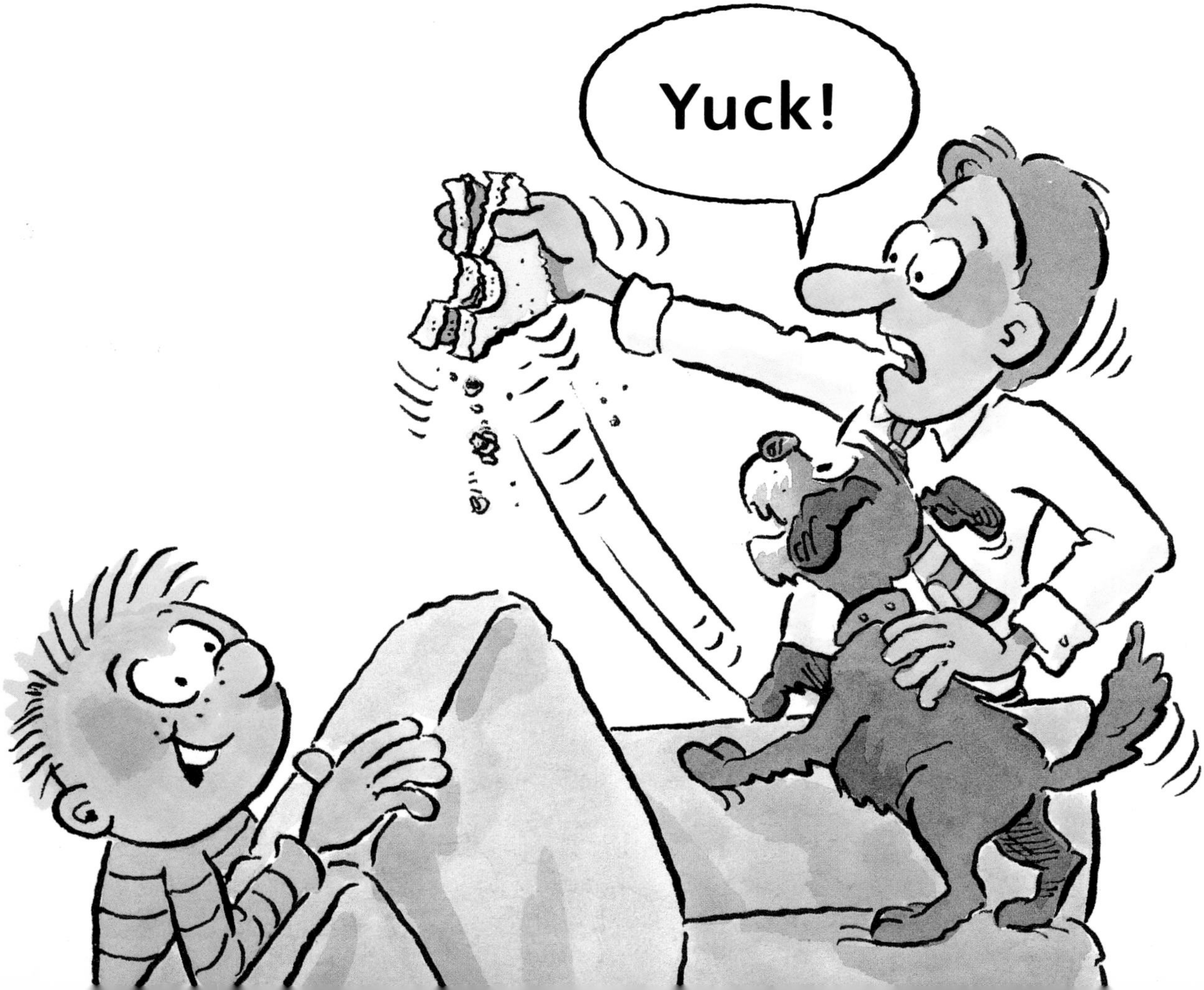